Text and illustrations copyright © 2003 by Lars Klinting
English translation copyright © 2006 by Maria Lundin
First published in English by Groundwood Books in Canada and the U.S.A. in 2006
Originally published as *Tuppen vill ha* by Eriksson & Lindgren in Sweden in 2003
10 09 08 07 06   2 3 4 5 6

Groundwood Books / House of Anansi Press
110 Spadina Avenue, Suite 801, Toronto, Ontario M5V 2K4
Distributed in the USA by Publishers Group West
1700 Fourth Street, Berkeley, CA 94710

Library and Archives Canada Cataloging in Publication
What do you want? / by Lars Klinting ; translated by Maria Lundin.
Translation of: Tuppen vill ha.
ISBN-13: 978-0-88899-636-7 (bound).
ISBN-10: 0-88899-636-5 (bound).
I. Lundin, Maria II. Title.
PZ7.K6625Wh 2004   j839.73'74   C2004-900973-7

Printed and bound in Denmark

WHAT DO YOU WANT?

LARS KLINTING

GROUNDWOOD BOOKS

HOUSE OF ANANSI PRESS

Toronto   Berkeley

The rooster wants…

his hen.

The bumblebee wants…

its flower.

Little brother wants…

his band-aid.

The hen wants…

her chick.

The chair wants…

its table.

The little old man wants…

his hat.

The bird wants…

its branch.

The little old woman wants…

her little old man.

The cone wants…

its ice cream.

The carriage wants…

its baby.

The fish wants…

its water.

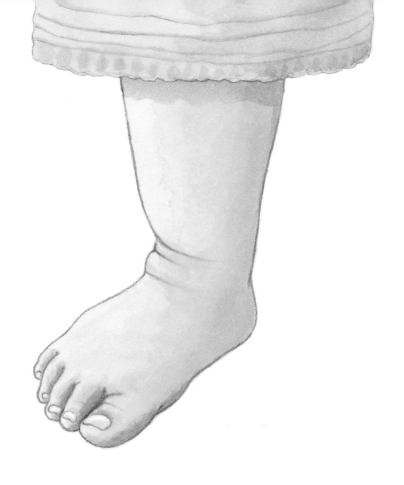

The foot wants…

its shoe.

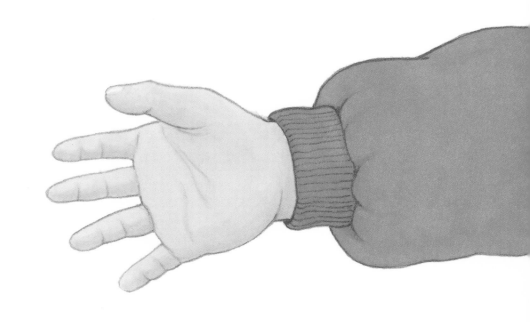

The hand wants…

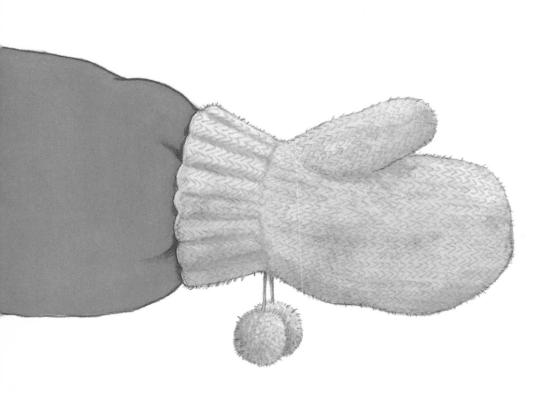

its mitt.

The teddy bear wants…

his friend.

The pillow wants…

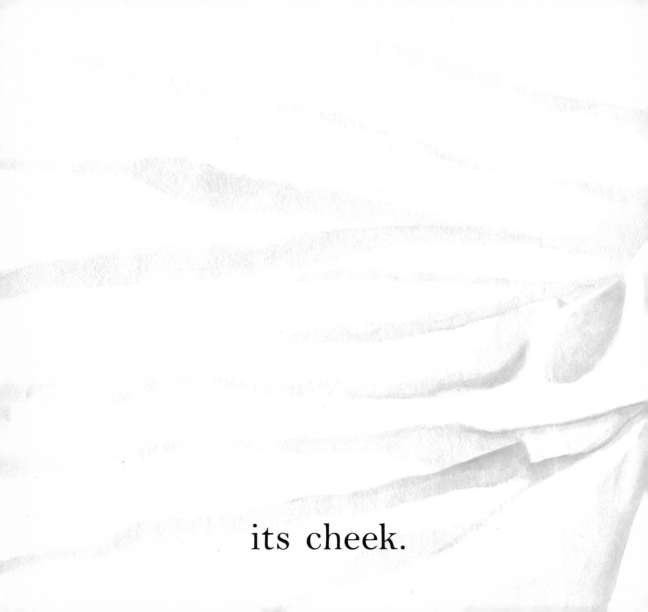

its cheek.